Rachel's  Library

Lev & Alla Revutsky

The Road to Parrot Country

Or the Curious Adventures of Rachel and her friends in Amazonia

San Jose * 2019 * San Jose

Lev & Alla Revutsky

The Road to Parrot Country

Or the Curious Adventures of Rachel and her friends in Amazonia

Illustrated by Vladimir Vitkovsky

Copyright © 2019 by Lev and Alla Revutsky

Dedicated to our lovely granddaughter,
Rachel Tilman

Rachel,

We wanted to write a little fairy tale for you, but then we quickly realized that girls grow quicker than books. Instead of a fairy tale, we wrote a story for you. We think by the time it is printed and bound you have grown old enough to read it. In the future, we hope that you will occasionally wipe the dust from this book and re-read it with your beautiful, charming smile, remembering Ava and Dida and how much they loved you.

BRASIL NEWS
CNN

TABLE OF CONTENTS

Chapter One

Rachel and Her Friends

At the edge of a forest near a small lake lived a red-haired girl named Rachel. Large pine trees and spruce trees grew in the forest, and their branches, like paws, shielded her little house from rain, wind and snow. In summer, Rachel collected flowers in the cool forest shade. She loved to put fresh flowers in her house to make it cheerful. She also collected berries and mushrooms to store for the winter. She often had guests for dinner and loved to give them her sweet raspberry or blueberry jam. Sometimes she treated herself with cookies smeared with jam.

The little house had just two bedrooms, a kitchen, where Rachel loved to cook, and a living room. Rachel shared her bedroom with Inga, a miniature Jack Russell Terrier with snow-white fur and one brown ear. Inga was her faithful companion and friendly to everyone.

The other bedroom held Gus, a big old grouchy parrot, and Kika, a nervous, energetic cat. At night, when Gus had trouble sleeping, he paced the room lost in thought or talking to Kika, who was tired and wanted to sleep. But she talked with Gus out of respect for his age.

In the living room, they had a bookcase, a TV set, a sofa, and a coffee table. In the evenings, they liked tea with jam while they watched their favorite shows. They especially liked to learn about animals, fish, and birds. Even grumpy Gus, who said TV was a waste of time, would doze off but sometimes sneak a peek at the screen.

Everyone had their chores around the house. Rachel gardened, cooked and shopped. Gus sorted through the mail, delivered the newspapers from the mailbox and dusted with a brush or a rag in his beak. Inga guarded the house, tagged along with Rachel to the store and helped pick mushrooms in the forest. Kika was the most organized. She oversaw the daily routine, made lists of things to buy, and planned the weekends. Whenever Rachel was gone, Kika followed Gus and Inga to make sure everything ran smoothly.

One Sunday after dinner, they watched a show about wildlife along the Amazon River. Gus fell asleep while Rachel petted Inga.

Suddenly, Kika jumped up, pointed at the screen and shouted, "Look! Look!" They saw a parrot just like their friend. "Gus, wake up!" they screamed. "You're on TV."

Gus looked up from under his wing and said, "Can't be. I'm here."

Inga ran back and forth from the sofa to the TV. How could her friend be on TV and on the sofa?

Rachel kept calm in the excitement. "How did you get there?" she said. Gus said nothing, but she felt something change in him when he saw those other parrots. What? she wondered.

"I'm sleepy," Gus said with a soft yawn and went to bed. Soon, the others stretched and went to sleep. But Rachel kept thinking about Gus and his mood.

Chapter Two

Gus's Sadness

*O*n the morning, everyone met for breakfast. Rachel loved to cook and did it well. She always served breakfast promptly at 8 a. m. with plates of their favorite foods. Gus liked his habits and ate the same porridge each morning. Inga loved sweet curd cakes. Kika liked just simple milk and biscuits.

It was a wonderful Sunday morning, except Gus was not there. Rachel thought this was odd, because Gus was always on time. When Gus finally came and sat down, he quietly picked at his food. To cheer him up, Rachel offered him his favorite biscuits and then candy, but he said no to both. "Just porridge," he said.

"Gus, are you feeling sick?" Rachel said.

"I'm fine," he said. He ate only half his breakfast and sunk into the sofa. Inga turned on the TV and said, "Come watch! Your hockey team is playing!" Gus never missed watching his favorite team. Now, he glanced at the screen, turned away and slumped back to his room.

"We have to do something," Kika said nervously.

"Let's bake his favorite pie with cabbage," Inga said. (She thought if Gus did not eat it, she could have extra pie.)

"I can make the pie," Rachel said. "But I'm afraid something serious is wrong with Gus. He needs more than a sweet pie."

"Let's ask a doctor, preferably a neurologist," Kika said. She read medical books, and everyone respected her opinion. "Maybe he needs regular exercise and vitamins."

"I will call Dr. O," Rachel said. "He knows Gus very well. He will know what to do."

What a relief. They were sure the wise old owl could help Gus.

Chapter Three

Doctor O Diagnoses Gus

Two days later, Rachel spent the day preparing a special dinner for their honored guest. Everyone loved old Dr. O. (His real name was Socrates G. Owl, MD.) The kindly doctor had lived in the forest for many years treating his neighbors. He sometimes saw patients in his house, a large oak tree deep in the forest. Usually, Dr. O visited patients at their homes to see how they lived and what they ate.

When he was not busy with patients, he read old medical books in Latin. He looked at the world through large round lenses in a frame he bought many years before when he studied medicine in France. Like many scientists, he was absent-minded and ignored daily chores and errands. Sometimes, he even forgot to eat.

The doctor's assistant, who helped him stay on schedule, was Nurse Owl. All the forest creatures were afraid of the older owl who never smiled. She wore a crisp white coat buttoned all the way to the top. While Dr. O kept his pockets full of candy and sweets for kids, Nurse Owl gave out only medicine and vitamins. She made home visits with Dr. O and made sure patients did exactly as he ordered. Behind her stern look, she had a kind heart. Like the doctor, she wanted the forest creatures to be healthy and happy.

When Doctor O and his nurse arrived, everyone rushed to greet them warmly and make them welcome. Rachel helped him take off his old, heavy coat and led him to the beautifully set table.

Dr. O's eyes and ears were weaker with age, but his sense of smell worked fine. He sniffed and caught the aroma of Rachel's meal of pea soup, homemade ravioli and cabbage pie.

"My dear," he said, "you should not have bothered yourself. A cup of tea is enough for me."

"No, no, Doctor. We saved the best for you," Rachel said.

Everyone sat at the table, with Kika next to the doctor. She always wanted to learn the latest medical news.

During dinner, while catching up with everyone and praising Rachel's cooking, Dr. Owl watched Gus. The old parrot looked sad, barely ate his food, and spoke little. He ignored his favorite cabbage pie. In the middle of dinner, Gus mumbled, "Please excuse me. Headache" and went to bed.

After dinner, everyone looked at Dr. O for his opinion. "Gus is unhappy about something," he said. "Kika was right." Kika blushed at his praise. "I think he needs a healthy change of place. A small trip, perhaps."
"But where?" Rachel said.

"Hmm. I must think about it and do some research," said the old doctor. Then he rose from the table, said goodbye to everyone and left the house.

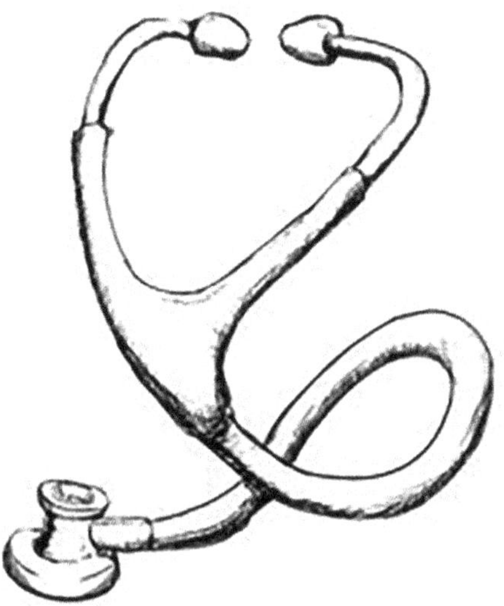

Chapter Four

Gus Tells His Story

Life in the house slowly got better. Doctor O gave Gus dandelion medicine and told him to exercise every day. Rachel made sure Gus put on his exercise clothes every morning and ran through the forest for 40 minutes. Inga ran along to keep him company. Two months later, Gus looked happier, had more energy and was more like himself.

"A healthy lifestyle has worked!" Kika said with pride.

"You are so clever," Rachel said with a kiss on her cold nose. "We are lucky to have you." Kika blushed and hid her face behind her paws.

One Saturday evening, Gus sat down at the dinner table and said, "My friends, I have news for you."

"I hope it's good," said Rachel, who did not like bad news. She felt grateful that bad news hardly ever came to their little house at the edge of the forest.
Gus held up a large yellow envelope with foreign stamps and announced, "I'm going to Amazonia!"

"But why?" said Inga.

"How?" said Kika.

"When?" said Rachel. None of them had ever traveled. All they knew about Amazonia came from books and TV: It is the largest country in South America, with quite different animals, plants and people.

"I have family there," Gus said. "Remember the show about Amazonia? That parrot you saw was my brother Charlie. I have not seen him for many years."

AIR P

The others were too shocked to speak. "Charlie and I got separated when we were two years old. When I saw him on the screen, I did not believe my eyes."

"I was right," said Kika. "He looked just like you."

"When we were young, people mixed us up. I watched the show over again until I was sure it was Charlie. After that, I wrote to the Amazonia government. They agreed he is my brother. I found his address and wrote him a letter. He has invited me to visit him."

Gus flapped his wings. He looked like his old self except not so grouchy.

Chapter Five

Rachel and Her Friends Take a Sea Voyage

The next day, while the friends sat at the table, Gus looked guilty. "I am sorry," he said. "I said nothing about Amazonia except to Dr. Owl when I saw him alone."

"Of course," said Kika. "Doctors keep things private."

"We all worried about you," said Inga. "I kept a close eye on you."

Rachel thought a moment and said, "Have you bought the tickets?"

"Not yet," said Gus.

"Fine," she smiled. "Let's all go together."

"Hooray!" cried Kika.

"We have not left the forest in a long time," she said, "especially together. Today I will buy tickets for all of us."

"Hooray!" cried Inga. She rushed to hug Gus, Kika and Rachel.

Chapter Six

Getting Ready For the Journey

everyone was eager for the big trip. They wanted to see Amazonia and reunite Gus with his family. After much talk they decided to go by sea. Rachel spent the money carefully and had saved enough to pay for everything.

The sailing was set for Sunday, and they were excited to prepare for the big day. On Friday, two days before the ship sailed, the organized house was a mess. Things were scattered all over. The friends buzzed with excitement. Kika was especially happy and delighted. She kept thinking of what to pack in her suitcase, the weather in Amazonia and what clothes were popular.

As a true gentleman, Gus needed only a few things. He fit everything into a small suitcase his parents gave him many years before.

Rachel made a list of what to bring to remember everything important. Inga ran errands, buying food for the trip and gifts for Gus's family. Kika made sure Rachel reserved a cabin for four with two portholes. She wanted it to be comfortable and roomy for their two weeks at sea.

After dinner that night, old Doctor O came by the house with his doctor's bag for visiting patients.

"I hope you have remembered to protect yourselves against illness," he said. "Who's first?" He saw panic on their faces as they thought of shots.

"It does not hurt at all," said Rachel. She felt afraid but wanted to look brave.

"I'll go first," Gus said, approaching the doctor. The owl opened his case and took out a chocolate bar. "But where's the shot?" he said.

"Shots are not needed now," Kika said. "Medical science has replaced them with sweets."

"Thank you," Dr. O said to Kika. "You said it perfectly."

The friends lost their fear and were happy to avoid a painful shot. Instead, they had chocolate and felt safe from getting sick.

Doctor O. bowed goodbye at the door and said, "I'll drive you to the port on Sunday. Be ready by 7."

Chapter Seven

The Adventure Begins

Sunday morning, when Dr. O. drove up in his old car, most of the luggage belonged to Inga and Kika. Rachel brought a light wooden box with homemade canned food as gifts for their new friends in Amazonia.

Gus stood ready with his small suitcase. Rachel wore a white traveling suit with a matching broad hat. Inga dressed in her sailor suit and cap. Kika slowly fanned herself under a pink umbrella. She had read some fashion magazines to see what passengers wear.

Dr. O. gave Rachel a box of medicines they might need, sandwiches from Nurse Owl and a list of herbs and plants to bring back from Amazonia.

The ship gave a loud whistle, everyone hugged the old doctor and hurried up the ramp. Soon the ship blew another whistle and slowly pulled away from the port. The ocean and the unknown Amazon lay ahead of them.

Chapter Eight

A Sea Voyage

As the ship moved away from the harbor, they gathered in their cabin. They looked out the portholes and wondered about their adventure. What would they see and do? What would they eat? Most important, what must they do to find Charlie? Soon Rachel turned away from the porthole and said, "We have a long journey ahead. We must keep busy."

"But we are on vacation," Inga whined. "We can afford to relax."
Gus and Kika said nothing. Each had their plans for the sea voyage. Gus had packed magazines and books including a small Amazonian dictionary and map. He wanted to learn the language and all he could about his brother's country.

Kika wanted to keep a diary of what she saw and learned plus travel notes. She planned to send reports to their daily newspaper, the *Forest News.* Kika's secret dream was to publish a book one day. Like Gus, she had a small language book.

Inga, the artist, planned to draw and paint. She had her easel and a box of colored paints in her suitcase. She hoped to paint the ocean, the floating islands and the sunsets. She also had a small book of language drills.

"Okay," said Rachel. "Rest a little, but then we must work on the language."

"All right!" said Gus as Inga and Kika unpacked their cases.

Every morning, after breakfast, they spent two hours on the upper deck studying Amazonian. In his free time, Gus read about the rain forest. Inga painted. Kika wrote her travel log and sent messages to the *Forest News*. Rachel practiced language.
The whole crew loved the travelers, especially Old Beaver, the captain. He wore a white naval tunic with an anchor insignia. He usually had a pipe between his teeth. He often sat with them at meals and told stories from his travels. One day he invited them to the deckhouse for a tour. He even let them steer the ship's wheel.

Rachel had many tasks to keep them organized. She sent everyone to bed on time and made sure they kept the cabin neat and tidy. Every morning, she arranged their meals with the ship's cook. With her extra language study, she taught the others what she learned on her own.

At first, everyone had difficulty with the language except Gus. He learned quickly, because it was his first language and came back fast.

"No wonder you're learning it quickly," said Kika. "You've always known it. Let's all try to speak only Amazonian."

On their thirteenth day at sea, Captain Beaver sat with the friends at dinner. "Tomorrow we will arrive at the port and have to part ways," he said. "Be careful and take care of yourselves. If you ever want to sail with me again, you are most welcome," he said as he left with a bow.

Later, they found a pair of old marine binoculars on the table with a note: *To Rachel and her friends, from Captain Beaver and the crew.* "What a nice captain," Inga said. "We must be polite and give him a gift from us. I have a seascape that will look nice in his cabin."

"Wonderful," Rachel said. "We can also leave him jars of jam and honey. There are strong winds around the ship. If the captain or one of the crew catches a cold, a spoonful of raspberry jam or honey is just the thing."

On their last night, they had mixed feelings. They felt sad to leave the ship but excited to see Amazonia and help Gus find Charlie. In the morning, when the ship arrived at the port, they warmly said goodbye to everyone. They hugged the old captain for the last time and went ashore.

Chapter Nine

First Day in Amazonia

tanding outside the ship terminal, surrounded by their luggage, they felt confused. Where to go? What to do first? "Gus, why hasn't anybody met us here?" Inga said. "Did you write Charlie our arrival time?"

"No. I wanted to surprise him," said Gus. "That was stupid, hunh?"

"But do you have his address?" said Rachel.

Gus took out his worn leather wallet and carefully looked through it, muttering to himself. "Ah, here," he said. He handed a paper to Rachel. "This is the address."

Rachel took the paper and read, "To make the cheese cakes add one tablespoon of sunflower oil to the dough . . . Oh, no," she said. "This is my recipe for cheese curds! You took it instead of the address. What are we going to do now?"

"It's okay" said Kika. "Stay calm. We just need to make a plan. We will not be lost." Everyone felt a little better at that. "In the meantime, let's eat. I cannot think on an empty stomach."

The friends agreed. As they looked for a place to eat, Inga said, "To learn a new country, start with a cafe."

"Food is the only thing that can comfort me now," said Gus.

They found a cafe and sat at an outside table. They admired the view, so different from their forest home. Instead of pines and spruce, they saw palm trees and eucalyptus trees. The buildings were bright and colorful not dark wood or stone. And the language sounded so different from what they read in their books. A waiter brought them menus. They read the words but did not recognize the new foods.

"When in doubt, order ice cream!" Inga said.

"Ice cream exists to be eaten," Rachel said, and she ordered a scoop of each flavor for the friends to share. A sweet first meal in Amazonia.

Chapter Ten

Searching For Charlie in Amazonia

When the friends finished their ice cream they went to the hotel. After showering and putting on fresh clothes, they still did not know how to find Charlie.

"Gus," Inga asked, "how will we look for him? What did he say in his letter?"

"I remember he lives in a small town by the Amazon River."

"Oh, my. That could be anywhere," she said. "Amazonia is very, very big. Maybe we should think some more and get a fresh start tomorrow."

They agreed and decided to explore the city. Near the hotel, they boarded a two-story tour bus that drove them past tall buildings in the city center, green parks, old buildings and beautiful churches. But they were used to the quiet, slow pace of the forest. The traffic and noise were new to them.

After a while, Inga said, "I would like living here." She jumped with excitement as she looked out the bus window.

"Not me," snorted Kika. "Life in the woods is much better. I would choke on the smog, and all that noise hurts my ears."

"Wait!" Rachel said suddenly. "I see a police station there on the corner. Maybe they can help us!"

When it stopped at the red light, they ran off the bus and into the police station. They saw a fat policeman dozing at a desk.

"Señor?" Rachel said in her best polite Amazonian. "Could you please help us?"

"Huh," muttered the policeman.

"Señor?" Rachel said again.

The policeman stretched, yawned and opened his eyes. He looked at the group in surprise and said, "Yes. Yes. How can I help you?"

"Mr. Policeman," bowed Gus. "We need big help." (Gus did not know how to say "difficult situation" in Amazonian.)

Gus, Inga and Kika all talked at once as they told the officer how and why they came to Amazonia that day and how they wanted to find Charlie who lived somewhere along the Amazon River. The fat policeman struggled to understand what these small foreigners wanted, but he listened carefully and took notes. Finally, Inga and Kika stopped talking. The policeman put down his notebook and bowed toward them.

"I believe these two charming Señoritas are saying that you, Señor, are looking for your brother. You think he lives in Amazonia, but you do not remember where?"

Gus nodded.

"Please sit down," the policeman said. "Coffee?"

The room was hot but Rachel and her friends were thirsty. They thanked the kind policeman and sat on the sofa. The office was a small room with two windows that had bars on the outside. It had a desk, two chairs, the old sofa and a safe. On the desk, the policeman had a stack of folders and an old black telephone. He drank from a small glass flask next to his phone.

"That is *matte*," said Kika. "Very popular in South America."

"I know," Rachel whispered. "It helps when you are hot or tired."

The policeman turned to Gus. "My name is Pedro. I will do all I can to help you. Please tell me everything about your brother, Charlie."

Chapter Eleven

Help from the Kind-Hearted Policeman

The policeman's name was Pedro, but the friends called him Don Pedro out of respect. Pedro made phone calls all over the country to ask about Charlie while the friends studied maps and telephone directories. With so many towns and settlements in Amazonia, they looked through many books and pages for Charlie's address.

Hours passed with no luck. Then the policeman said, "Dear friends, we cannot do all of this in one evening. You must be tired and hungry. Please come home with me for dinner. My wife will be happy to receive you."

Rachel looked at her friends. They were tired, but excited to see an Amazonian family.

"Thank you for your kind offer, Don Pedro. May we stop by the hotel first?" Rachel wanted to get homemade honey and jam to bring as a gift.

After a quick stop at the hotel, Don Pedro drove them in his roomy car. His house sat on a quiet street away from the city center. Several orange trees gave shade to the front. Along one side were garden beds full of vegetables.

Don Pedro's wife, Donna Flora, met them at the door. The beautiful Señora kissed everyone on both cheeks and sat them at a long table covered with baked and fried pasta and fish plus cheeses and fruit. Rachel smiled at so much fresh food.

The hungry travelers eagerly ate a large supper. Kika and Inga yawned and nodded off to sleep. Don Pedro carried them to the sofa. Donna Flora poured strong coffee for Rachel and Gus.

Setting down her cup, their hostess said, "What is your plan to find Charlie and his family?"

"Let's go over it again," Pedro said. "My job as a detective is to get all the facts. The smallest details are important."

As they talked over the lives of Gus and Charlie, an hour passed. Inga and Kika awoke from their naps. When his wife was not watching, Don Pedro took more marmalade. More time passed into the night.

Chapter Twelve

Midnight in Amazonia

ust after the clock struck midnight, the doorbell rang. A small balding man stood on the doorstep. His eyes were smiling and bright, but he moved nervously.

"This is my friend, Señor Vittorio," said Pedro. "He is a very experienced officer."

"He is also my brother," said Donna Flora. She kissed Vittorio on both cheeks.

"Very nice to meet you, Don Vittorio," said Rachel.

"No need for the ceremony," Vittorio said. He sat down and helped himself to meat and bread. "I am not a Don to you. I am old Vittorio. And this fat man, my best friend, is just Pedro," he said while chewing. "At work, we are Dons but here, at little Aunt Flora's house, we are all friends."

Then he jumped up from the table, ran to embrace Pedro, then the friends. He talked nonstop and swallowed between words. Finally, Vittorio fell into his chair and drank a cup of *matte*.

Soon he said, "I think I know where Charlie lives." Vittorio held out a piece of paper to Pedro. In large letters it said *Papagaios City* just below Charlie's name.

"Papagaios!" said Don Pedro. "I know the place." He laid out a map on the table and took a red pencil. "Unfortunately, the road to Papagaios is rough and dangerous."

Donna Flora said, "These little ones should not be allowed to go there alone."

"You are right, as always," Pedro said. "We are thinking the same thing."

Don Pedro drew more red lines on the map while Vittorio wrote numbers in his notebook. They looked at each with serious eyes. "Excuse us," Vittorio said as they left the room. When they returned, Vittorio said, "According to our numbers, you will need at least two weeks to get to Papagaios."

"If everything goes smoothly," said Don Pedro.

"Oh, these men!" Donna Flora threw up her hands. "Stop wasting time and get to the point. These two sit in their offices all day and do nothing."

Turning to Gus and Rachel, she said, "We cannot let you go alone. You need protection."

"Thank you so much, Donna Flora. What shall we do?"

"Nothing now. Sleep here tonight, and we will get moving in the morning." The house had several empty bedrooms, and the weary travelers fell asleep when their heads hit the pillows.

Chapter Thirteen

Donna Flora and The Friends Plan a Trip

n the morning, Gus awoke first. He hopped downstairs to find Donna Flora in the kitchen.
"What's the plan?" he said. "What's our next move?"

She scowled at the parrot. "Your next move is to the patio," she said.

"The patio?"

"Yes. Sit there and have coffee while I make breakfast."

"But . . ."

"No buts. In Amazonia, first we eat. Then we talk. After that we think and then we act."

The rest of the group came downstairs and followed Gus outside to sit under the trees. Rachel volunteered to help with breakfast. She watched closely as Donna Flora made *empanadas*, Amazonian patties. In turn, Rachel cooked her own specialty, cheesecakes.

Thirty minutes later, plates of cheesecake and *empanadas* sat on the table in the shady part of the courtyard. Donna Flora served her own snow-white sour cream, while Rachel added her homemade berry jam. Donna Flora also offered banana jam and guava jam. Everyone drank fragrant Amazonian coffee, which they all grew to love. The hungry group ate everything on the table.

"I will get fat very quickly," Inga said between bites of *empanadas*.
"Everything is so delicious," Kika sighed, switching bites between the cheesecake and flat patties.

Gus ate a little and kept talking with the two policemen while pouring himself a third cup of coffee. The three bent over the map to find the best route.

"So," Donna Flora said firmly, "you need a big car, or even a police bus with plenty of room for everyone. Do you have a bus to rent in your precinct?"

"You mean Giuseppe," said Vittorio.

"Old Giuseppe will not refuse to join you," Donna Flora said.

"Auntie Flora, you should command an army," laughed Gus.

"I have commanded but not without challenges," said Donna Flora. "Do you think I spent all my life in a kitchen, feeding this slacker and his children?" She lightly stroked her husband's back. "No, my friends. I worked at the department for 20 years. I was even the boss of these two guys!" she said.

"And you are still commanding," Vittorio said. He winked at Pedro.

Donna Flora announced again that Vittorio and Pedro must go with the friends to guide and protect them. She kissed her guests goodbye and stood waving in the doorway until Vittorio's car was out of sight.

Chapter Fourteen

The Friends and the Bus

When Vittorio drove into the police yard, the old bus was dozing in the sun. He had already served his time, running more than one million kilometers. When he retired three years before, the police department gave him the honor of the best parking spot.

The right and left sides of the engine hood were painted with medals he received for his long service in the police department. He had been repainted and shined up nicely, but a close look showed the bus was an old model. Near the rear bumper they saw traces of bullet holes. A few small dents on the sides showed his heavy fighting service.

The bus rarely left the garage now except to ride in a parade or a carnival. On those days, the old bus transformed himself, looking young and shiny like other honored buses. The rest of the time he was in quiet retirement.

Vittorio put his finger to his lips. "This is our old man," he whispered, touching the side of the brown bus. "My old friend. We traveled many roads together."

Then Vittorio tapped lightly on the hood. "Wake up, old chap. Look who I brought you."

The old bus woke up in a gesture of welcome, gave a brief honk and blinked his headlights. "To whom do I owe the pleasure?" he said.

Rachel and her friends bowed and waved to the bus.

"I am Guiseppe," he said. "Retired Master Sergeant Bus at your service."

"Old man, we need your help," said Vittorio.

"You remember me only when you need me," he grumbled. "You and your friend Pedro."

"For some jobs, you are the only one we trust." Vittorio knew he had to flatter the old sergeant. "When we need you, only you can do the job."

"True enough," he said. "I earned these medals you see up here."

Vittorio gave a respectful pause. Then he said, "We have not come empty-handed." He held up a large bag of Donna Flora's carefully prepared delights: homemade sausages, cheese, cookies, juicy red tomatoes, and a thermos of hot coffee. Rachel had added her curd cakes.

The old bus smiled. "Flora is a holy woman. If not for her, I would completely forget the smell of homemade food."

"This is all for you," Pedro said. "We just came from Flora's house."

"That explains all the food," Giuseppe laughed.

Giuseppe ate some of Donna Flora's food and neatly folded the leftovers into a little bag. After a final sip of dark coffee, he said, "Well, old buddy, how can I help you?"

Vittorio spread out the map and said, "Gus and his friends must go to Papagaios to find his brother. Here is the route we have planned. As you can see, it is many days of rough riding through jungle and mountains. No other bus knows those roads the way you do. For safety sake, you are the one for the job."

Giuseppe sat silent while thinking. Rachel felt desperate and hugged the old bus. "Please, dear Giuseppe," she begged.

Giuseppe looked at everyone, winked at Rachel and said, "If someone needs old Giuseppe, he is happy to help."

"Hooray!".

"I need 12 hours to get ready," he said. "Come back tomorrow morning at 6 sharp. I will be in the garage. We must start in the cool of the morning. Tell Auntie Flora to pack food for us, especially her famous *empanadas*. That is my only condition."

"Everyone else must get ready in the meantime," commanded Vittorio. Then he said goodbye to the old bus and drove Rachel and her friends to their hotel.

Chapter Fifteen

Traveling to Papagaios

At 5:30 a.m., Pedro and Vittorio drove up to the hotel. Small Vittorio and big Pedro had two boxes of Donna Flora's food with them. They wore plain clothes, but the outlines of their weapon holsters showed under their shirts. Pedro laughed at their surprised looks.

"These are not real. We are only allowed to carry service weapons while on duty. These are sports pistols, which we brought just in case."

"Can I have one?" asked Gus. Pedro winked at Vittorio and handed Gus a sport pistol.

"Well, I hope nothing happens to us on our trip," Inga said. "I have a show of my paintings waiting for me at home."

Rachel hugged Inga and said, "Relax, darling. We will all come to your show."

Bus Giuseppe met them at the gate. He looked beautiful, clean and sparkling with shiny new tires. Pedro and Vittorio loaded all their supplies into the back of the bus.

After breakfast, Pedro said, "We must have a secret name for our group."

Rachel counted heads and said, "We are four plus Pedro and Vittorio. That makes six."

Inga said, "Don't forget Giuseppe. He makes seven."

"We are the Magnificent Seven!" said Kika.

"Great," said Giuseppe. "I like the Magnificent Seven."

"Now that we have a group name, let's divide the work," Vittorio said. "Old Giuseppe drives. Pedro and I keep the group safe. Gus and Inga follow the route and choose where we rest and sleep. Kika will watch the money and make sure we have enough gas, food and water. She will also keep the trip log for a report to our general."

"The general is my wife," said Pedro. Everyone laughed.

"Yeah, we all know that," said Vittorio. "We also need to choose a commander."

"Rachel, of course," said Pedro. "She is the best commander."

Inga and Kika clapped and hugged Rachel. "Yay. Our Rachel can solve any problem!"

"Let's vote," said Gus. "Who votes for Rachel?" Everybody but Rachel raised a hand.

"Who is against?" No one voted against Rachel.

Kika wrote on the first page of a large notebook in her neat handwriting, *The general meeting of the travelers all approved Rachel as commander of the group, the Magnificent Seven.*

Rachel blushed and said, "I agree, but only if you all help me. And now, it's time to leave. We have a long trip ahead. Kika, make a note in the logbook, June 5, 8 a.m. departure."

"Hurray!" they cried again and clapped their hands. Old Giuseppe blinked his headlights and gave a long beep. The engine came to life and the bus pulled away from the police garage. With that, they were off to find Charlie.

Chapter Sixteen

Adventure on the Way to Papagaios

When they left the police garage, Guiseppe drove them through the new part of the city. They saw many tall buildings and wide roads with cars rushing here and there. Soon they entered the narrow streets of the old city, where many people sat at sidewalk cafes. Some read newspapers while they drank coffee or cold drinks. Others played chess or dominoes. The friends watched as old city life went by out the windows.

"Everyone looks so happy," Gus said. "Is it always like this?"

"We are a happy country," said Pedro. "We love to have fun."

"Except when people break the law," said Vittorio. "That is serious business."

They settled into their seats as the bus rolled out of the city into the countryside. To pass the time they practiced Amazonian, read books or listened to Pedro, Vittorio and Giuseppe tell stories. Rachel also told the policemen about their life on the edge of the forest.

That first day they stopped for gas in a small town. Rachel saw a strangely dressed man sitting at a low table with cards, small rods and a dish of gray, green and red stones. "Pedro, what is that man doing?"

Pedro looked up from his card game with Vittorio and peered out the window. He saw the old man in the long colorful robe with feathers in his hat. He wore a necklace with large colored beads. "Him? He looks like a fortune teller."

"Do people do that here?"
"Village people believe their healers can foretell the future. They come into the towns on market days. It's nonsense, but many people give them a little money and enjoy it."

"Wow," said Rachel. "I wish I knew my future."

Vittorio looked quickly at Pedro and spoke to Rachel. "Ha! Pedro is an old fat fool. I have the gift of telling the future."

Pedro rolled his eyes and folded his arms.

Vittorio said, "Rachel, come here, dear. Give me your left hand. It will show me the signs of your future."

She reached out her left hand to him. He looked at her palm, turned it over and looked at her knuckles, then her palm again. Then he sniffed her hand, closed his eyes to concentrate and said, "Yes, yes. I see it! Many trees around you. . . But I see darkness in your future, too, and fatigue. You will be very tired. . . Wait. It's OK. I see stars that will guide you."

"Ha, ha, ha," Pedro burst into wild laughter. He slapped his partner in the chest.

"You old liar. That's not her future. That's tonight in the jungle after a long day. We've had no rain, so the stars will be out." Rachel blushed but laughed, too.

"Shame on you, fooling a little girl like that."

Vittorio said, "Wait. You will see that all I said will come true." Vittorio winked at Rachel.

Three days passed and the road ran into a rainforest. They had never seen so much thick green life and so much color. Their mouths fell open when they saw the high ferns, flexible creepers, palm trees, and rubber wood, all new and strange.

The forest seemed like a fairytale to them. Birds of all colors and sizes flying around or nesting in the trees, giant anteaters, jaguars, snakes hanging from tree limbs, giant lizards and more, all living together. They saw giant water lilies with leaves two meters across growing along the Iguazu River. They were most amazed by the huge cannon trees with fruits resembling cannonballs. When the fruit fell to the ground, it looked and sounded like a cannonball hitting the earth.

The friends were most impressed by the Iguazu River. In the waters they saw a frightening kind of alligator with a huge mouth and many sharp teeth. Dozens of colored birds flew over their heads. Pedro and Vittorio reminded them never to go alone into the dangerous jungle.

"After the Nile River in Egypt, this is the longest river in the world," Kika said.

"On our next trip," said Rachel, "maybe we can go to the Valley of the Nile."

Hour after hour they passed through small towns and villages. Sometimes, Giuseppe stopped in a central square. While the bus refueled and rested in the shade, the friends and their police escort walked around town, going to local shops and markets to buy food and drink.

One week into the trip a late afternoon rainstorm washed away the road. Until the road reopened, they had to stay overnight in a hotel.

Giuseppe settled down for the night in a warm, dry garage while the others unpacked their things and went down to the restaurant. The room was small and crowded. They were tired, cold and hungry, so they ordered the biggest pizza on the menu.

At a nearby table two men sat. From their clothing and faces, Rachel thought they looked dirty and troubled. On their table was a half-empty bottle of wine. When they saw the group of six, the men got up and introduced themselves.

"I am Archibald or Archie," said the taller one. He was balding and combed his few hairs to one side. His eyes were drooping, which made him look sleepy. He pointed to his companion and said, "This is Leopold or Leo," who kept silent. They looked scary and unpleasant.

Archie and Leo did not wait for an invitation but moved their chairs and sat down with the group. Both policemen felt uneasy. They wanted to get rid of the nasty-looking men, but Rachel whispered, "Don't worry. We're OK."

Archibald grabbed a large slice of pizza and swallowed it. Then he ate a second piece. Inga, Gus and Kika watched the pizza disappear in what seemed like a circus performance. They had never seen anyone eat so fast. They guessed Archie had not eaten well for a long time. When he finished the pizza, he drank a large mug of cocoa, then closed his eyes.

Leo had been quiet at first, but now he talked and smiled at everyone. He asked Gus about his life, gave compliments to Inga and Kika, and praised the way Rachel had organized the trip.

They grew tired of his nosy questions and wanted to send the two pests on their way. Gus joked that he had received a lot of money from his family and was in a hurry to give millions to his brother's family in Alenquer. "I hired the two best policemen in the world to protect us," he said, pointing to Pedro and Vittorio.

When Archibald heard "money" and "police," he perked up. With no more food on the table, he got up and returned to their table. Leopold followed him.

"What a weird couple," Rachel said.

Kika said, "They did not thank us or say goodbye."

"I have a bad feeling about them," Pedro said. "Tomorrow I will ask the local police about them. They look like thieves. Gus, no jokes about money, please. They came to our table for a reason."

Gus was sorry for his joke and worried that he had let down his friends.

"I did not like them, either," said Inga. She and Kika tried to overhear what they said at their table, but the room was too noisy.

Vittorio used a small camera to take several pictures of Archie and Leo. He wanted to know who they were and whether they were criminals known to the police.

"We must get out of here right away," Rachel said, looking at the two rude men.

The next morning, when they came down to the restaurant, they did not see Archie and Leo. The rain kept falling but lighter than the night before. They planned to leave right after breakfast.

While the friends ate breakfast, Pedro and Vittorio rode Giuseppe to the police station. They returned an hour later with serious faces.

"Good news but bad news," said Pedro. "Good detectives learn what we want to know. Those two are wanted for prison escape. Their records show multiple robberies. Archibald, the boss, likes to break into cars and apartments. He also robs people on the street."

"His accomplice, Leopold, is a very skillful cheat," said Vittorio. "He uses a friendly manner to make people trust him. Then he tricks them into giving him money for nothing."
"A disgusting couple for sure," said Gus. "I failed you all. I'm an old fool."
Vittorio said, "We suspect they might follow us."

"We need to leave immediately," Rachel said.

"Let's get Giuseppe. The weather has cleared. Now is a good time."

"Is there another way to Papagaios?" said Inga.

"Alas, no," said Pedro. "But do not worry. There are seven of us. We are the Magnificent Seven. Among us are two professionals. We will handle them just fine."

"True," Vittorio said. "But maybe these crooks know other bad guys who will help them."

"Let's get going," Giuseppe said as he arrived at the hotel entrance. The two policemen had told him about the strange pair. "Load the luggage, sit down and we'll leave."

Giuseppe and the group headed toward Papagaios. In the evening, near dark, they stopped for the night. With no towns or villages nearby, they set up a small camp along the road. When they sat down to have dinner, they heard strange sounds from the forest.

"It sounds like someone crying for help," said Rachel. Everyone rushed to investigate. The sounds stopped as suddenly as they began.

"Let's get back to the camp," said Pedro. Approaching the camp, Inga said she saw a brief, moving shadow. The friends listened carefully, but all was quiet. They heard only the firewood crackling as it burned and the snoring of old Giuseppe.

"The tea is ready," Gus said as he poured it into mugs.
Rachel sipped her tea, yawned and slowly fell asleep. All the others did the same, sipped their tea and nodded off. Kika and Inga drank hot milk and stayed awake.

"What happened to them?" Inga wondered.

"Very strange," said Kika.

"Let's let them sleep," Inga said. To feel safe, they took the pistols from Pedro and Vittorio, who were also sleeping.

Thirty minutes passed. Inga and Kika were alert when two figures slipped out from behind the bushes: Archie and Leo. Pedro was right! The thieves thought the friends were rich and easy to rob.

Archie knew only one narrow road ran to Papagaios and the Magnificent Seven would be easy to find. He and Leo rode a motorcycle from the hotel before sunrise and hid in a small gorge. When the bus stopped for the night, they set out to rob them. Leo made the cries for help while Archie slipped into the camp and put sleeping powder in their tea. Inga and Kika did not drink the tea and stayed awake, but the robbers were not prepared for that.

Kika and Inga were calm when they saw the bandits. Inga wanted to pull a pistol on them right away (the bandits did not know the pistols were fake), but Kika wanted to wait. So they hid behind a tree and watched.

Archie and Leo took out ropes and gags and tied up the sleepers. Then they sat and warmed themselves at the fire. Leo took out wine while Archie opened a basket of food.

"Let's have a bite and find the bags of money," Archie said with his mouth full.

"Take it easy," said Leo. "Money never escapes us. I wonder where the other two have gone."
"That makes no difference to us," Archie said. "The fewer the better." They laughed at their easy success while they ate and drank.

Rachel, Gus and their two guardians were tied up but soon began to stir awake.
They were groggy and struggled weakly against the ropes.

Just then Inga and Kika jumped out from behind the tree with pistols in their hands.

"Hands up!" ordered Kika

"Don't move," shouted Inga, aiming the gun at Leo.

Leo dropped the wine bottle, and Archie coughed and choked on a piece of bread. Caught by surprise, they had no idea what to do. By then, Gus used his sharp beak to cut Rachel's ropes, and she untied the gag in her mouth.

Archie and Leo panicked and ran toward their motorcycle. Inga and Kika threw the fake pistols at the robbers. One hit Leo in the head. He fell down and got knocked out. The other gun missed Archie, who ignored Leo and kept running. He jumped over the tied-up policemen, who could only watch.

Speedy Rachel grabbed Archie's feet. He lost his balance and fell. Inga and Kika jumped on him and tied his arms and legs. Archie lay weak and still. He knew his plot with Leo had failed. Gus hopped with his feet bound and pecked at Archie's right ear which made him cry out in pain. Inga and Kika untied Pedro and Vittorio and helped Rachel to her feet.

When she threw herself at Archie's feet, Rachel scraped her knees and scratched her left eyebrow. Kika sat her down and gave first aid. She rinsed Rachel's wound and covered it with a bandage. The eye patch made Rachel look like a pirate.

Even though the thieves wanted to rob and hurt them, the friends felt sorry for them. Rachel and Kika treated their wounds and gave them medicine. Both had small cuts on their faces, and Archie's right ear was red and swollen from Gus's brief attack.

They made Archie and Leo prisoners under a tree. The police put handcuffs on them and tied their legs with rope so they could not get away. But what to do with them? Pedro was firm. He would not set them free, and no one wanted to leave them out in the jungle.

"We have to take them with us on the bus," he said. "We can hand them over to the police at the next station."

Chapter Seventeen

Adventure Continues on the Road to Papagaios

The friends continued their journey with Archie and Leo riding with them on the bus. Now they had two more grown men to feed, and Archie eating as much as two people. Their food supply was shrinking fast along with their money. The robbers' old clothes were destroyed, so they bought new pants, shirts and sandals for Archie and Leo.

With new clothes, enough food to eat and a dry, comfortable bus to ride on, the thieves behaved well. They also looked like most people in Amazonia. As the group rode along, Rachel studied mathematics and history with them. Gus taught them to play chess, and Vittorio and Pedro taught them some law. In turn, Leo showed them card tricks.

At each stop, Archie and Leo helped the friends with shopping and keeping the bus neat and clean. They seemed like new men who had learned from their mistakes. They also liked the way the friends treated them with kindness, which was new to them. When they promised not to escape, Pedro and Vittorio said it was safe to remove their handcuffs.

At the next large town the bus stopped at the police department. Two local officers took Leo and Archie off the bus. Their sad faces said what everyone knew: they must return to prison. When Rachel said goodbye to Leo and Archie, she gave them some money and jam. She also gave them two large notebooks, pens and envelopes.

"If you behave and write to us every week, maybe we can visit you," she said. All the friends hugged the two enemies who were now friends. They all had a rare sad moment when the Magnificent Seven left for the highway leading to Papagaios.

The seven were happy to be on their way again. But now Rachel and Kika had a new problem to solve. They had enough money and food for only three more days, but they needed another seven days to reach the end of their journey.

The next day, after breakfast in a roadside cafe, Rachel did not want to give them the bad news. Kika sat next to her with the log of the trip and the record of how they spent the money. Before Rachel spoke, excited Kika jumped up and said, "We're almost out of money."

"And food," Rachel added sadly.

"No matter," laughed Vittorio. "Anything good can happen. One time, Pedro and I waited for three days to capture some bandits. All we had to eat were two packs of biscuits, two tiles of chocolate, water and *matte*. This fat man did not even lose weight," he said, gesturing to Pedro.
"Did you catch the bandits?" Inga said.

"Of course we caught them. That was easy."

"Then what happened?"

"The hardest part was to keep the fat man awake and make sure he did not steal my food," Vittorio said with a laugh.

"Chatterbox," Pedro said.

"In fact, my brother-in-law Pedro is a hero. If not for him, I would not be here with you."

"Enough memories," Pedro said. "We need to get money for food and gas."

Vittorio had them empty their pockets. They put all their bills and coins on the table. Now they had just enough to buy gas and food for four days, but only if they spent very carefully.

"Who has suggestions?" said Rachel.

The table was quiet while Gus looked at the local newspaper. Soon he shouted, "Eureka! We can work to make some money. There are plenty of jobs here for everyone."

Gus showed them the ads for workers. The small town was near a huge forest full of rubber trees. Locals called Hevea the Tree of Life. They could work as rubber pickers in the forest. The Magnificent Seven hopped on the bus and went to apply for jobs.

Chapter Eighteen

The Friends Go to Work

*S*oon they found the office of the rubber company and were quickly hired. Their work began the next day. Until then, the company had them watch a training video on how rubber is drawn from the trees, processed in a factory and made into many useful things. They were fascinated by how local people used the natural world to help them survive and live well.

The company also sent them to a house run by a kindly husband and wife. When they got to the house, the aroma of food was wonderful. After a long day of applying for the jobs and training, they were very hungry, and the food smelled delicious. The kind husband and wife prepared several dishes they ate every day: an aromatic soup made of beans, sweet potatoes and other vegetables, and soft and tender flat cakes baked from cassava flour.

Most of all, the friends loved the dessert: cream-mousse from acai berries and candies from the exotic fruit of coupu. The most delicious food they had ever eaten. To thank the host couple, Inga painted their portrait, a new experience they had never imagined.

Everyone in the town, including the elderly couple, lived their lives connected to rubber. The elderly man had learned to master his father's skill which he taught to his children. The old latex picker worked all year round, leaving for the forest early in the morning and returning at twilight. Collectors covered an average of twenty kilometers per day walking from tree to tree.

The worker's wife worked with other women in a small factory, where the sap of the rubber trees was processed into a semi-finished rubber. The sap of the Hevea gave work, and therefore life, to generations of native Amazonians. So they called Hevea the tree of life.

The next morning, eager to start, everyone went to work. Rachel, Kika and Inga stayed with the women to work in the village. Giuseppe took the policemen and Gus into the woods, where the locals and the latex collectors were waiting for them. In the forest, only men worked as collectors. Because, the police and Gus were new to Hevea, they were given the simplest tasks.

Collectors cut a neat groove on the tree, and the latex drained down into a special bucket. Pedro, Vittorio and Gus walked around the trees to make sure the buckets were filled almost to the brim. Then they carried the buckets close to the road where they emptied them into a big vat. Pedro and Giuseppe drove the full vat to a small factory where the women worked.

At the factory, Rachel, Kika and Inga helped others clear the latex of dirt and added water and other special ingredients. After the latex got thick, the women passed it through a manual press, creating neat, even layers of rubber. The layers were dried for eight days and then sent to factories to be made into many different, useful things.

The first day was very difficult for everyone. The work was simple, but they were not used to intense labor. Their hands and feet ached. At dinner near sundown, they had little energy for talk. They ate, took showers and fell into bed. Tomorrow was another working day, and they had to eat and be at work by 7 a.m.

Chapter Nineteen

A Lost Friend and Frightening Spider Bite

By their fifth day on the job they had adjusted to the routine of rubber work. That morning when Kika awoke she said, "I feel like I have been living here for a very, very long time."

"Yes" said Rachel. "I feel the same. What a surprise."

There were only a few days left to work, when they had new troubles. The collectors were sent to a new part of the forest, farther from the town. Rachel had warned everyone that Gus is absent-minded and asked them to watch him. Until then, Gus was always in sight, working together with Vittorio or one of the natives.

But that day, Gus fell behind. He got distracted by a large heron. He had never seen something so gorgeous so close to him. He stopped to chat with the beautiful bird and fell behind the other pickers. Time passed. When he realized he was behind, he rushed to catch up with everyone, but they were out of sight.

When Gus thought he could not catch up with the group, he tried to find his way home. He did not know where to go. Parrots can both walk and fly, but during life with people, Gus forgot how to fly. He did not try, because living in the forest with Rachel, Kika and Inga, he did not need to fly.

"I must try my best to take off," he thought. He tried and tried but rose only a few centimeters. He "flew" for about one second, then fell back on the ground. Gus tried to take off again and again, but he could not fly. Disappointed, he sat down on the ground in the shadow of a big tree. Soon he was fast asleep.

Gus did not know how long he slept. He awoke with a feeling of being pushed. He opened his eyes and saw a huge snake, an anaconda, looking at him with curiosity. Gus froze, and the first thing that occurred to him again was to try to pretend he was asleep, then maybe the snake would lose interest and leave him alone. Gus closed his eyes, covered himself with a wing and thought, "Whatever happens, I hope I end up okay."

The anaconda looked at Gus, swayed slightly and made hissing noises. Those few seconds seemed like forever for poor Gus. When the hissing stopped Gus opened his eyes. The snake was not hungry and silently slithered away.

What a relief! His lucky escape gave Gus more strength. From the shock of nearly getting eaten, his heart pounded hard inside his little chest, and he took off in flight, determined. He rose above the rainforest and followed the road that led to the village.

At the same time, the factory where Inga worked was closed for lunch in the middle of the day. Like everybody, Inga worked from early morning until early evening. Usually at lunch, Rachel, Inga and Kika went back to their house, where they rested in the midday heat before returning to the factory.

But Inga wanted to go into the forest for a quiet hour of painting. People warned them that walking alone in the forest was not safe. The natives in the forest knew every path, but even they never went into the jungle alone.

Inga's curiosity overcame her fear. At the edge of the forest, she settled under a tree and took out her easel and brushes. She had waited so long for this moment ever since they talked of seeing the beauty of the rain forest. For the first few minutes she could not draw. She felt the beauty around her so strongly, her hand would not move to draw lines. How to show the beauty of nature with art? Instead, she just sat in peace, admiring her surroundings.

She felt a sharp pain in her paw. Afraid and hurting, she dropped her paintbrush. A huge spider, more than 7 centimeters wide, had bitten her.

Fortunately, the thick wool on her paw softened the bite, and it did not go deep beneath the skin. Still, it hurt a lot. She grabbed her supplies and struggled to get back to the village.

Rachel and Kika were at home. They rushed Inga to bed, her paw already swollen, and Rachel searched for the antidote that would reverse the poison. Kika grabbed a bike and rushed to find the local healer. In the village, news spread quickly, and soon Pedro and Vittorio arrived to help.

Fortunately, Dr. O had also packed an antidote for spider bites in his medicines. Inga swallowed two bitter tablets. After a few minutes, she felt less pain. Rachel bandaged Inga's paw, and together they waited for the healer. Inga dozed off but did not sleep long.

Soon, Kika and an old man entered the house. Rachel could not tell how old he was. His hair was very white, and his skin was tanned and wrinkled. But he stood up straight, and had muscles on his arms like a younger man. He had a sparkle in his eyes, too. From his lips, there hung a straw rolled from grass with smoldering ashes.

The old native leaned toward Inga, removed the bandage and examined the wound. Then he washed the wound with a strange green liquid and covered it with ashes from the tube. He took from his bag a bright resin ball the color of blood. The old man chewed the resin and put it on the wound but did not cover it. Finally, he had Inga drink a large cup of hot liquid, which tasted like fruit tea.

"Your friend will sleep until morning," he said. "When she wakes, she will be healthy. Your doctor's medicine and our herbs will restore her in 12 hours."

"I will give you some resin balls, but you may not need them. Take them to your doctor. Tell him how we treat wounds here." He handed Rachel a small package with leaves and balls of the red resin. Later, their hostess told Rachel the resin came from a tree the locals called the Dragon Tree.

 "How can we thank you?" Rachel said. "You saved our Inga!"

The old healer smiled. "Come visit us again. When you return home, tell your friends about our way of life."

They all felt relieved. But soon they had another scare. Gus walked through the door. In the madness of Inga's bite, they did not know he was missing, since he usually worked late. He told everyone his adventure with the large snake.

Try as he might, Gus still could not fly as he had. Even an image of the anaconda could not make his wings raise him more than a few centimeters off the ground. Gus felt sad to think he would never fly again.

All's well that ends well, they thought. Inga slept peacefully, and everyone was safe together. Their stay with the rubber company ended.

Chapter Twenty

Parting with the Village

n the morning, Inga woke up feeling great. Her wound had healed with only a small dot showing.

The friends had promised to work for the company for two more days. As before, they rode to and from work on old Giuseppe. When everyone was seated, Giuseppe said, "Friends, I have news to give you. I am sorry. I promised to be with you until the end of your journey. But I want to stay here."

They were shocked but silent.

"For many years serving in the police, I dreamed of retiring to somewhere in nature. I have loved our time here, and I don't want to leave. I will not be idle. I will take local children to school and help these wonderful people."

"But we need you," Rachel exclaimed in a cracking voice. "How will we finish our journey without you?"

Kika was near to tears. "Giuseppe, please don't desert us now."

"I have thought of that. You will be fine without me, I promise. An hour's drive from here is a small pier. Twice a week a little boat stops there. It makes a two-day trip to Papagaios. The boat is beautiful, and you can swim in the great river. It will be far more pleasant than being in the old bus."

Then old Giuseppe turned away and large drops appeared on the windshield, although there was no rain in the sky.

Kika burst into tears first then Inga and Rachel. The old parrot, Gus, turned away with a lump in his throat.

Pedro stood silent, also confused and surprised. Vittorio rescued all.

"You will not get rid of us forever," he said. "Don't think it. We will all come visit you. And for this group," pointing to Rachel and her three friends "no ocean will stop them."

Rachel nodded yes.

"I'm happy for you, old man," Vittorio said. "You deserve peace and a good climate. If you ever miss our adventures or fatty Pedro, come back to us at the police station. And there is always Donna Flora's cooking." Giuseppe smiled and blinked his headlights.

Rachel stepped to Giuseppe and pressed her cheek to his warm side.

"And let's give something to Giuseppe so he will always remember us!" Kika said. "Inga can paint portraits of us on each side of the old bus. Wherever he goes, Giuseppe will always have us with him."

"Well done, Kika!" cried Rachel. Old Giuseppe blushed.

The next two days passed easily. They kept working and spent the evening with their new friends. They talked, ate and laughed among the people. Inga painted their portraits on Giuseppe's side panels.

The last day arrived and the town arranged a farewell dinner celebration for Rachel and her friends. With much food and dancing, still they were sad to leave. They had made friends with the locals, worked with them side by side and learned how to collect rubber in the jungles of Amazonia.

Kika wrote all this to the *Forest News*, ending with, "Best of all, we were lucky to spend a week with lovely people in a most beautiful place across the ocean."
Only their goodbye with Giuseppe made them sad.

Chapter Twenty-One

Family at Last

On departure day they collected all their luggage and loaded the bus. Giuseppe drove them through the village. Giuseppe's sides were painted with colorful portraits of the Magnificent Six. (Inga wisely decided not to paint a portrait of Gus on the side of Gus.) Locals stopped the bus to give them gifts and baskets of food.

The wife of the old healer who treated Inga brought gifts for them. Rachel, Kika and Inga received colorful beads, the same as the women wore in the village. An elderly woman said, "These beads protect you from disease and other troubles."

Pedro, Vittorio and Gus received native knives carved with designs of animals, symbols and the sun, the moon and the stars.

Embracing the wife of the healer, Rachel felt how hard it was to say goodbye to the lovely local people. She knew them only a short time, but she loved their warm smiles and the way they lived in harmony with the land. In the forest, Rachel never parted with her friends. Now she and her friends had to leave the kind people of this beautiful town they were lucky to call home for a week.

Giuseppe slowly rolled down the road. Everyone felt sad, because in a few hours they would have to say goodbye to him, too. Pedro, Vittorio and Donna Flora could visit Giuseppe, but Rachel, Kika, Inga and Gus knew they were parting from the old bus for a long time, maybe forever. Everyone felt a heartbreak.

To cheer up the group, Giuseppe turned on an Amazonian samba song. That helped their mood but only a little.
Giuseppe had to say something. "My friends, I'm too young to die yet. Remember, I am in retirement. In a year or two, I will be able to travel to you. That is, if you still remember old Giuseppe." Hearing this, everyone's mood improved.

Giuseppe then drove them to the town by the pier where the boat waited for them. Rachel, Pedro and Vittorio went to buy their tickets. When they returned, everyone hugged old Giuseppe one last time and climbed the ramp to the deck.

After the third whistle, the boat sailed slowly away. The farther it went, the smaller Giuseppe looked. His friends waved to him for a long time, until at last they could see him no more.

Two days later the ship tied up at the port of Alenquer in Papagaios. Rachel and her friends breathed freely. They had reached their goal. They crossed the ocean, went through many wild adventures, and met many new friends along the way: the wonderful Pedro and Donna Flora, the merry fellow Vittorio and, of course, Giuseppe.

When they walked down the ramp from the boat, a cheering crowd of parrots greeted them. Before they had time to look back, they found themselves in the arms of Gus's loud, dancing relatives, who looked exactly like him. As though they were in a whirlwind of an Amazonian carnival, they circled the friends, ending their greeting with fireworks and soap bubbles. Spying his brother in the crowd, Gus ran to him excited and happy at last.

"Charlie!"

"Gus!"

No words could express the joy of two brothers embracing.

To Be Continued . . .

ПОПУГАЙОС
ГОША

Acknowledgements

In the process of preparing and writing this book, authors have received an unwavering support and encouragement from many people: family, friends, artists, book editors, and translators. It would be impossible to mention all of those who inspired us and contributed to the creation of this book; however, we would like to at least note a few of them.

Dr. Lewis Osofsky aka "Dr. O" is Rachel's physician since she was born. "Dr O", together with Dr. Jacob Revutsky, (one of the authors' grandfather) served as the inspiration behind the characted of Doctor O.

Dennis Briskin -- English version editor -for his exemplary literary skill and unparallel attention to manuscript. His editing was crucial to make English version of the book the way it is now.

Vladimir Vitkovsky for his excellent work in creating wonderful book illustrations.

Michael Gershzon - editor – for his Russian-version editing and excellent ideas on how to improve the book.

Arkady Levit – for his thoughts and suggestions on how to make this book more appealing to young readers.

Maria Revutsky-McDermott was instrumental with her ideas and English language proofreading. The important discussions we had, helped us with the concept of the book.

Mary Tilman was critical with literary assistance and draft editing. Her knowledge of children literature was very helpful while we worked on the draft of the book.

Eugene Tilman has taken an important role as a technical and business manager, allowing us to concentrate on writing.